HELPING YOUR BRAND-NEW READER

Here's how to make first-time reading easy and fun:

▶ Read the introduction at the beginning of each story aloud. Look through the pictures together so that your child can see what happens in the story before reading the words.

▶ Read one or two pages to your child, placing your finger under each word.

▶ Let your child touch the words and read the rest of the story. Give him or her time to figure out each new word.

▶ If your child gets stuck on a word, you might say, *"Try something. Look at the picture. What would make sense?"*

▶ If your child is still stuck, supply the right word. This will allow him or her to continue to read and enjoy the story. You might say, *"Could this word be 'ball'?"*

▶ Always praise your child. Praise what he or she reads correctly, and praise good tries too.

▶ Give your child lots of chances to read the story again and again. The more your child reads, the more confident he or she will become.

▶ Have fun!

First edition 2007

Library of Congress Cataloging-in-Publication Data is available.

Library of Congress Catalog Card Number pending

ISBN 978-0-7636-2963-2

2 4 6 8 10 9 7 5 3 1

Printed in Hong Kong

This book was typeset in Letraset Arta.
The illustrations were done in acrylic on paper.

Candlewick Press
2067 Massachusetts Avenue
Cambridge, Massachusetts 02140

visit us at www.candlewick.com

Larry and Rita

CANDLEWICK PRESS
CAMBRIDGE, MASSACHUSETTS

Jamie Michalak ILLUSTRATED BY Jill Newton

Contents

Rita Blows Bubbles

Introduction

This story is called *Rita Blows Bubbles*.
It's about how Rita keeps blowing bigger
and bigger bubbles, until finally she
blows away!

Rita blows a bubble.

4

Pop!

Rita blows a big bubble.

6

Pop!

Rita blows a bigger bubble.

8

Pop!

Rita blows the biggest bubble.

10

Rita blows away!

Larry and Rita Dance

Introduction

This story is called *Larry and Rita Dance.* It's about how Larry and Rita dance together—until Larry's sharp spikes poke Rita. Ouch!

13

Larry dances.

Cha, cha, cha.

Rita dances.

Cha, cha, cha.

Larry and Rita dance together.

18

Cha, cha, cha.

Ouch!

Larry and Rita dance apart.

Rita at the Fair

Introduction

This story is called *Rita at the Fair*.
It's about how Rita plays a ball-tossing
game at the fair. But instead of hitting the
bottles with the ball, she hits Larry!

Rita throws a ball.

She hits one bottle.

Rita throws another ball.

26

She hits two bottles.

Rita throws another ball.

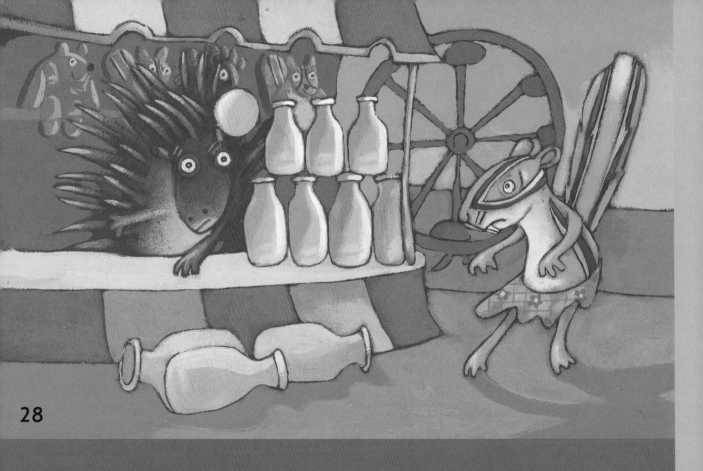

28

She hits Larry!

Larry hits all the bottles.

Rita wins a doll!

Larry and the Crab

Introduction

This story is called *Larry and the Crab*. It's about how Larry grabs things at the beach and puts them in his pail. But then Larry picks up a crab and the crab grabs Larry!

Larry grabs a shell.

He puts it in his pail.

Larry grabs a rock.

He puts it in his pail.

Larry grabs a starfish.

He puts it in his pail.

Larry grabs a crab.

The crab grabs Larry!